There

Marie-Louise Fitzpatrick

A NEAL PORTER BOOK
ROARING BROOK PRESS
NEW YORK

A Neal Porter Book

Published by Roaring Brook Press

Roaring Brook Press is a division of Holtzbrinck Publishing Holdings Limited Partnership

175 Fifth Avenue, New York, New York 10010

www.roaringbrookpress.com

Distributed in Canada by H. B. Fenn and Company, Ltd.

Cataloging-in-Publication Data is on file at the Library of Congress

ISBN-13: 978-1-59643-087-7

ISBN-10: 1-59643-087-7

Roaring Brook Press books are available for special promotions and premiums.

For details, contact: Director of Special Markets, Holtzbrinck Publishers.

Printed in China

Book design by Jennifer Browne

First edition May 2009

2 4 6 8 10 9 7 5 3 1

For Bernardine, with love

When will I get There?

How will I know?
Will there be a sign that says,
"Here is There"?

Will it take long to get There?

Till tomorrow?

Till next week?

Next year?

Will I be really BIG, There?

As tall as a house? As tall as the trees?

Will I never be too small again?

Will I wear sensible shoes
and say sensible things?
Will I never say anything
silly again?

Never,

ever,

ever,

ever?

What color are sunflowers, There?
Are blueberries still blue?

And will there be rainbows?
I'll still build snowmen and sandcastles.
Definitely.

And will I know everything, There?
Will I know all the secrets?
Will I know how to count the stars
and how to fix the broken things?

Is it a jungle, There?

Will I find my way through?

Will there be dragons?

Will they be really fierce?

Do you know how to tame dragons?

I do.

You look them right in the eye and count to ten,

then they just fly away.

Can Teddy come too?
Can I stop along the way?
Can I pick daisies?

Is everybody going There?

Can I change my mind
and go Elsewhere instead?

I won't go today.

I've got lots to do.

I'll go There tomorrow.

Definitely.